HIP-HOP

Alicia Keys
Ashanti
Beyoncé
Black Eyed Peas
Busta Rhymes
Chris Brown
Christina Aguilera
Ciara
Cypress Hill
Daddy Yankee
DMX
Don Omar
Dr. Dre
Eminem
Fat Joe
50 Cent
The Game
Hip-Hop: A Short History
Hip-Hop Around the World
Ice Cube
Ivy Queen
Jay-Z
Jennifer Lopez
Juelz Santana
Kanye West

Lil Wayne
LL Cool J
Lloyd Banks
Ludacris
Mariah Carey
Mary J. Blige
Missy Elliot
Nas
Nelly
Notorious B.I.G.
OutKast
Pharrell Williams
Pitbull
Queen Latifah
Reverend Run (of Run DMC)
Sean "Diddy" Combs
Snoop Dogg
T.I.
Tupac
Usher
Will Smith
Wu-Tang Clan
Xzibit
Young Jeezy
Yung Joc

Juelz Santana is a young newcomer with a lot of promise. Fans and critics are anxious to see how far he can go in the music world.

Hip-Hop

Juelz Santana

Janice Rockworth

Mason Crest Publishers

Juelz Santana

Copyright © 2008 by Mason Crest Publishers. All rights reserved. No part of this publication may be reproduced or transmitted in any form or by any means, electronic or mechanical, including photocopying, recording, taping, or any information storage and retrieval system, without permission from the publisher.

Produced by Harding House Publishing Service, Inc.
201 Harding Avenue, Vestal, NY 13850.

MASON CREST PUBLISHERS INC.
370 Reed Road
Broomall, Pennsylvania 19008
(866)MCP-BOOK (toll free)
www.masoncrest.com

Printed in the United States of America

First Printing

9 8 7 6 5 4 3 2 1

Library of Congress Cataloging-in-Publication Data

Rockworth, Janice.
  Juelz Santana / Janice Rockworth.
     p. cm. -- (Hip-hop)
  Includes index.
  ISBN 978-1-4222-0297-5
  ISBN: 978-1-4222-0077-3 (series)
  1. Santana, Juelz--Juvenile literature. 2. Rap musicians--United States--Biography--Juvenile literature. I. Title.
ML3930.S265R63 2008
782.421649092--dc22
  [B]
                                        2007032962

Publisher's notes:

- All quotations in this book come from original sources and contain the spelling and grammatical inconsistencies of the original text.

- The Web sites mentioned in this book were active at the time of publication. The publisher is not responsible for Web sites that have changed their addresses or discontinued operation since the date of publication. The publisher will review and update the Web site addresses each time the book is reprinted.

DISCLAIMER: The following story has been thoroughly researched, and to the best of our knowledge, represents a true story. While every possible effort has been made to ensure accuracy, the publisher will not assume liability for damages caused by inaccuracies in the data, and makes no warranty on the accuracy of the information contained herein. This story has not been authorized nor endorsed by Juelz Santana.

Contents

Hip-Hop Time Line	6
1 Hip-Hop's Newest Artist	9
2 Music with History	21
3 The Early Years	29
4 Out on His Own	37
5 Still a Rapper	49
Chronology	56
Accomplishments and Awards	58
Further Reading/Internet Resources	59
Glossary	61
Index	62
About the Author	64
Picture Credits	64

Hip-Hop Time Line

1970s DJ Kool Herc pioneers the use of breaks, isolations, and repeats using two turntables.

1970s Grafitti artist Vic begins tagging on New York subways.

1976 Grandmaster Flash and the Furious Five emerge as one of the first battlers and freestylers.

1982 Afrika Bambaataa tours Europe in another hip-hop first.

1980 Rapper Kurtis Blow sells a million records and makes the first nationwide TV appearance for a hip-hop artist.

1984 The track "Roxanne Roxanne" sparks the first diss war.

1988 Hip-hop record sales reach 100 million annually.

1985 The film *Krush Groove*, about the rise of Def Jam Records, is released.

1970   1980

1970s The central elements of the hip-hop culture begin to emerge in the Bronx, New York City.

1974 Afrika Bambaataa organizes the Universal Zulu Nation.

1979 "Rapper's Delight," by The Sugarhill Gang, goes gold.

1981 Grandmaster Flash and the Furious Five release *Adventures on the Wheels of Steel*.

1983 Ice-T releases his first singles, marking the earliest examples of gangsta rap.

1984 *Graffitti Rock*, the first hip-hop television program, premieres.

1986 Run DMC cover Aerosmith's "Walk this Way" and appear on the cover of *Rolling Stone*.

1988 MTV premieres *Yo! MTV Raps*.

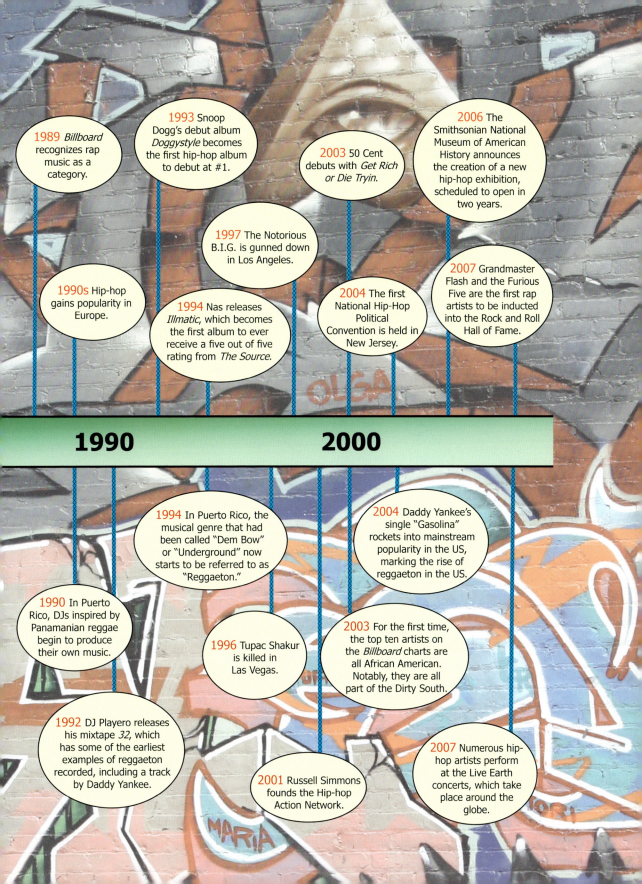

Juelz Santana may be one of hip-hop's newest artists, but he's hit the scene with a bang. He's proved to be a crowd-pleasing rapper and a savvy businessman.

1

Hip-Hop's Newest Artist

Most people his age are working day jobs or graduating from college. They are pondering career moves, further education, and the possibility of starting a family. They are paying off student loans and saving for a down payment on their first condo or house. But while his peers are thinking about beginning their adult lives, Juelz Santana has other thoughts on his mind. He's worrying about record deals and chart positions. He's signing autographs for fans and making public appearances. And he's spending his hours laying down tracks in the studio and hoping for a top-10 hit.

A Rapper and a Businessman

Juelz Santana is only in his mid-twenties, and yet he's one of rap music's rising stars. Since his late teens, he's been making a name for himself with guest appearances on other rapper's albums, numerous *mixtapes*, and two solo albums of his own. He's also an *entrepreneur* with a keen eye for business opportunities. His efforts as a hip-hop artist have won him a growing fan base and spurred other ventures, including clothing lines, a store called Santana's Town, and the vice presidency of Diplomat Records. Even with all these other accomplishments, however, Juelz is still best known for his music.

Juelz Santana has a slight build and boyish face, but don't be fooled. His style is anything but light or innocent. With a voice that's surprisingly deep and biting, he raps about drugs, gang life, and violence. His songs are filled with profanity and sexually explicit lyrics, and his music definitely isn't for everyone. In his lyrics, he's a gangbanger, a drug dealer, and a pimp, although he does throw in dance tracks and a few raps about love and family along the way. But most of his songs are tales of selling crack, getting high with friends, and shooting enemies. He even has songs and skits with lyrics about slapping women. In a review of Juelz Santana's most recent album, *What the Game's Been Missing*, for sixshot.com, the article's author, Premiere, describes Santana this way:

> "While appearing to be no more than another **homophobic**, drug-dealing rapper to the untrained eye, Juelz Santana is instead one of the most likable personalities within the hip-hop industry today."

Clearly Juelz is complicated and controversial. Nevertheless, in his short career, Juelz has gained a lot of fans, and he's now confirming his position as a force in the music industry.

Juelz is a hip-hop artist, but that term isn't very descriptive since there are many types of hip-hop music. Some might call him a gangsta rapper, since lyrics often discuss being a "gangsta." Gangsta rap is one of the most hardcore and controversial styles of music around. In gangsta rap, the beats are typically dark and heavy. The music is gritty and usually created with a technique called sampling, in which pieces (samples) are taken from other recordings and mixed together to create the new track. The lyrics are filled with profanity, violence, and criminally oriented themes.

Although many of Juelz's songs would fit the gangsta rap category, that label is usually reserved for artists from the West Coast. East Coast artists with similar styles and subject

Hip-hop music has been criticized for lyrics filled with violence, hatred, and profanity. But it's also been criticized for glorifying a life filled with excesses—money, parties, clothes, jewelry, women.

matter are usually called hardcore hip-hop artists. But while some of Juelz's songs seem gangsta or hardcore, many other songs discuss lighter or more personal themes. Musically speaking, Juelz Santana's songs tend to be more radio and club friendly with lighter beats. Samples, especially in his first album, are often taken from **R&B** songs, rather than the grittier samples that define gangsta rap. But Juelz's lyrics are very gangsta and hardcore oriented, so some people might be tempted to define his music as "pop-gangsta" for the way it mixes gangsta lyrics and pop-oriented music. Juelz, however, would probably reject that label since it comes with a lot of unflattering baggage.

A Hardcore Style

Juelz may hail from the East Coast, but he says that his earliest influences and hip-hop heroes were Tupac Shakur (a West Coast rapper) and Scarface (a Southern rapper). He is also clearly influenced by the gangsta rap style. Gangsta rap began in the mid- to late eighties. The heart of the early gangsta rap music was South Central Los Angeles, an area filled with gangs and gang violence. Hip-hop artists coming out of that area, like Ice-T and N.W.A., pioneered gangsta rap music with heavy beats, samples, and hardcore lyrics filled with profanity, violence, and gang-related themes. The music shocked many people, people who couldn't understand what redeeming value the music could possibly have. But the new musical style also quickly gained a big fan base of people who either identified with the life rappers rhymed about or simply enjoyed the music.

Many gangsta rappers defended themselves against the critics by saying they were simply revealing the realities of inner-city life. Many saw themselves as messengers of the truth—a truth filled with stories of **oppression**, poverty, violence, and police brutality. Often gangsta rappers seemed to glorify gang life in their songs. But some gangsta rappers also pulled political and social messages into their lyrics, educating their listeners about the terrible conditions of the ghetto and mourning the realities there. Furthermore, gangsta rappers often portrayed their characters as heroic victims: people who were born into the poverty-stricken ghetto with no hope for a better life through law-abiding means, and who took matters into their own hands and earned a living through whatever means necessary (even if those means were gangs, drugs, and criminal behavior).

As gangsta rap's popularity grew, however, the political and social messages began to fade, and the glorification of gang life increased. "Bling" became the new thing. Gangsta rappers spit rhymes about their cars, clothes, diamonds, and women—all bought and paid for with drug money, blood money, gangsta "business," or rap money. Much of the music also changed, becoming lighter, more radio friendly, and designed for popular consumption. This lighter music was intended to be played on the radio and sold in record stores, rather than passed around on the **underground** street scene. Critics charged that the new gangsta music was different from what it had been in the past. They said it was now concerned only with "bling-bling"; with partying with lots of women, being adored by fans, and being feared by other gangstas and MCs. Some people called this new type of gangsta rap "pop-gangsta."

Gangsta vs. Pop-Gangsta

Juelz would argue with being labeled a pop-gangsta artist, because many people are critical of the pop-gangsta style. When some people say pop-gangsta, they only mean that the music mixes gangsta themes with popular music styles. But other people use the term as an insult, charging that pop-gangsta music is inauthentic and doesn't "keep it real." They say that

JUELZ SANTANA

Gangsta rap has had a major role in hip-hop music. One of its pioneers was Ice Cube. Today he's probably better known for his starring roles in many films, including *Are We There Yet?*

gangsta rap grew out of real-life situations and real-life problems, but that pop-gangsta rap turned the music into a money-making machine concerned with nothing but bling.

Hardcore gangsta rappers also criticized the new pop-gangsta rappers for posing as something they were not. They said pop rappers rhymed about gang life and violence, not because they had a whole lot of experience in that area, but because the music sold and they wanted to cash in. Some people say the difference between gangsta rap and pop-gangsta rap can be described this way. While the original gangsta rap had a lot of controversial lyrics and themes, it often encouraged its listeners to think about the causes and trappings of inner-city life. In pop-gangsta rap, that thoughtful element is generally gone; the music is all about the party.

None of this is to say, however, that pop-gangsta rap isn't a legitimate form of music. After all, the **genre** still has legions of fans and sells millions of records. Pop-gangsta rappers say that their music is about entertainment, and that there's nothing wrong with giving fans the entertainment they demand. Of course, many parents, journalists, academics, and members of the public disagree. Gangsta rap, whether in its more traditional or its newer pop-oriented form, offends many people. "Parental advisory" stickers grace its album covers, and many people argue the lyrics ultimately encourage violence, racism, sexism, and give all hip-hop music a bad name.

Where Juelz Stands

Juelz Santana would bite back at such claims. His songs might mix gangsta lyrics with more club-friendly music, but he doesn't see himself as a rapper just making music for the *mainstream*. In fact, in an interview with Tom Breihan for the *Village Voice*, Juelz spoke out against rappers who make their music simply for mainstream consumption. He identified the practice as part of what is wrong with today's hip-hop music, and said that rappers need to maintain a closer link with their fans:

> "There's a lot of [rappers] right now that ain't keeping it as real, ain't doing the type of [stuff] we be doing and representing the way we be representing. If they want New York to be where it needs to be, then [rappers] need to work hard. . . . I'm doing what's real to me, what comes to my heart. I feel like a lot of people in New York, that's what they're not doing. They not doing what comes to they heart and what they really want to do."

Juelz believes that doing the hard work to create good music means listening to yourself as an artist and listening to your fans. He believes you need to know who your fans are and what they want to hear. To do that, he believes artists need to go out into "the hood" and stay in touch with the public. In the same *Village Voice* interview, he also talked about how important his fans are to him, and how he is not one of those rappers who just records in a studio. He lives and walks the streets, and he says that's what keeps his music authentic and real. After a performance, he often goes out and spends time with fans, signing autographs and having pictures taken with the people who adore him:

> "I get real motivated when I be out and I do a performance. . . . I know what it's like to be a fan, to just look up to somebody like that. People think stars are so hard to reach and so hard to touch. When I'm out, especially in the hood . . . I got to give that love back. I feel like I'm amongst the same kids I grew up with on the block . . . I represent them. I'm the voicebox of the youth right now, today's average teenager becoming a man, the same [stuff] he's going through, the hustle,

HIP-HOP'S NEWEST ARTIST   17

Juelz believes it's important to keep in touch with the people. After all, rap is supposed to be about the real world. So, when he's not recording or working on his other projects, Juelz hits the streets, checking in with the people who live that reality every day.

the struggle, the situations you get put through to go through life. People struggle everywhere. People are poor everywhere. People deal with pain and hurt and [stuff] everywhere, so that's what I get across."

Juelz definitely feels that his music is the voice of his generation, and in many ways he's absolutely right. Whether you love it or hate it, gangsta rap, hardcore rap, and other hardcore styles are popular and influential around the world. And

Hip-hop music, including some of its more controversial forms, is no longer just an American phenomenon. It's become one of the most popular genres all over the world.

whether you consider rappers like Juelz Santana to be great artists or not, they are definitely front and center in the hip-hop world today. While it sometimes seems that people have nothing but criticism for today's hip-hop music, not all hip-hop music is so controversial. In fact, if you had listened to hip-hop music in its earliest days, you probably never would have guessed the huge waves it would make in the future. Hip-hop began as simple party music. Today, artists like Juelz Santana are just the newest generation participating in a musical tradition that dates back to the 1970s and has roots that go back even further.

Hip-hop didn't just spring up out of nowhere. It has a deep history, especially in African American music. One of its ancestors is R&B, and one of that genre's biggest talents is the legendary BB King—and his guitar, "Lucille," of course.

2

Music with History

Music is an important part of virtually every human *culture* on earth. It has played a particularly important role in black American culture from the very earliest years. The very first black people in North America were brought here as slaves, and racism and oppression have been a defining part of life in America for black people ever since. As black American culture developed, music became an important way to psychologically combat racism and oppression. In the days of slavery, black people sang spirituals to raise their spirits and pray for freedom and salvation.

Protest Music

After slavery ended, the tradition of music as a defining part of expression and resistance in black culture continued. On its

Web site at www.pbs.org, the PBS program *Independent Lens* refers to the era from the end of the Civil War until the mid-twentieth century as dominated by a "Southern campaign of racist terror," stating:

> "According to the Center for Constitutional Rights, between 1882 and 1968, mobs lynched 4,743 persons in the United States, over 70 percent of them African Americans."

In this period, black culture continued to use music as an important means of expression, as well as a means of educating the public (both black and white) about the extreme racism and oppression. Blues was a sorrow-filled music. Jazz was a music that raised people's spirits. Perhaps one the most dramatic examples of music as a tool of protest, however, can be seen in the song "Strange Fruit." Written in the 1930s, its lyrics depict the South as a land filled with "fruit"-laden trees, the gruesome fruit being the dead bodies of lynched black men. The song was actually written by a Jewish man, Abel Meeropol, from the Bronx, New York City. But it was most famously sung by Billie Holiday.

Through the power of its words and Holiday's voice, the song became an anthem of resistance and educated many people about the plight of black Americans and the deadly racism they faced. That tradition of music as an inspirational, educational, and revolutionary tool would only continue and grow, and by the 1970s, the tradition would manifest itself anew in a type of music called hip-hop.

Keeping the Tradition Alive

When hip-hop music first developed, it was all about dancing and having a good time. It started in the Bronx in the 1970s, when DJs began using two turntables to cut and mix beats for dance parties, which were very popular in the black and

Latino neighborhoods. While the DJs spun records and mixed beats, they "toasted," or called out, to the crowd. Soon MCs took toasting to a new level by rhyming over the DJ's rhythms. They rhymed about anything that came to mind, but the most common topic was the MC's skills. The style was called rapping, and the foundation for all hip-hop music (mixing beats and rapping) was laid.

From the Bronx, hip-hop music exploded out into other parts of New York City. Then it spread to other cities around the United States. The new music was especially popular in the inner city, where rapping became a way for poor and frustrated young people to express their thoughts and feelings. It also became a way for young people, especially teenage and twenty-something males, to earn respect. Rappers battled each other at parties, on street corners, and at clubs. The audience cheered, booed, hollered, and proclaimed the winner of the battle. Freestyle battles, in which the rapper made up rhymes on the spot, were the greatest test of a rapper's skills, and a good freestyler could gain a lot of local and even regional fame.

Hip-hop, however, wasn't just about music. The music was just one part of a much larger developing street culture. Hip-hop culture was an urban street movement that consisted of music, dance, and art, and it inspired its own attitudes, fashion, and language. Like DJing and MCing, break dancing was an important part of hip-hop culture. Break-dancers would spread out old cardboard or scrap linoleum at train stations, corners, or parks. Then they'd get down to hip-hop beats, busting crazy moves, displaying fancy footwork, and spinning on their backs, shoulders, and heads. Those radical break-dancers inspired all kinds of additional forms of street dance, which over time would become the hip-hop dance styles we know today.

Tagging (or graffiti) was also a big part of inner-city life that would become a defining part of hip-hop culture. Taggers

JUELZ SANTANA

Hip-hop is about more than music. From the beginning, graffiti artists—taggers—put their mark on almost anything that didn't move. Some people call it art. Others call it vandalism and a crime.

earned local fame by throwing names like Cornbread, Taki 183, and Tracy 168 up on walls, bridges, subway cars—just about any place they could "get up" and be seen. To many people, graffiti was just vandalism that disrespected property owners, brought down neighborhood values, and encouraged crime. But to other people, graffiti was a way to rebel, get famous, and express themselves. Taggers developed complex styles, and some people even began to see graffiti as a legitimate form of public art. The urban murals became a defining part of inner-city life, and graffiti styles have influenced many other art forms.

The music, dance, and art that began in New York's inner city spread around the country. The music also moved beyond the streets, appearing first on urban radio and ultimately making its way to popular stations. From that original party music, multiple hip-hop styles were born, and like black music throughout history, many had important political and social messages.

The Spread of a Revolution

By the 1980s, hip-hop music was moving around the country and had gained an image as being "black music." That image has never been completely accurate, for from the very beginning, hip-hop has had artists and fans from many *ethnic* backgrounds. Latino artists have been particularly involved in hip-hop music from the beginning. But its reputation as black music does have a basis in some real circumstances. After all, hip-hop was the music of the inner city, and because of historical inequalities, inner-city populations were largely black.

So hip-hop music developed to reflect and represent many aspects of black culture and concerns of black communities. Like Billie Holiday singing about lynching in the South, MCs began rapping about poverty, crime, drugs, police brutality, and other topics that plagued their communities. Different hip-hop styles developed, including political hip-hop,

JUELZ SANTANA

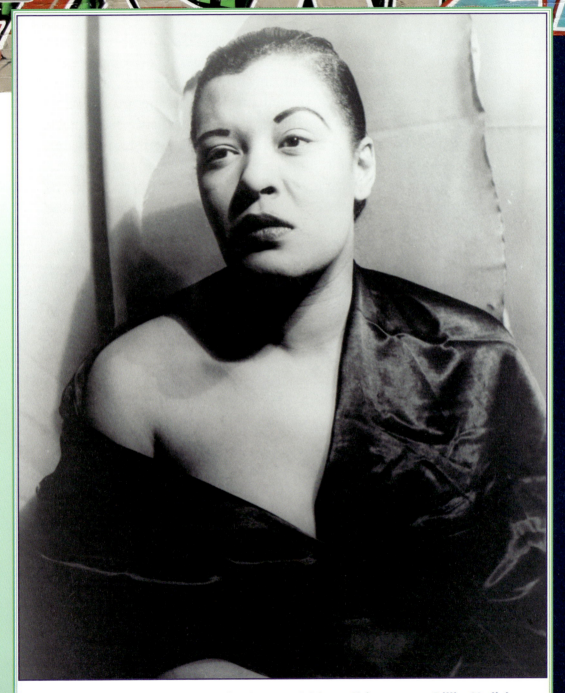

Music about what's wrong in the world is nothing new. Billie Holiday, for example, sang about lynching in the 1930s song "Strange Fruit." That song, and others like it, helped educate people about what was going on in the real world.

conscious hip-hop, Latin rap, and gangsta rap. The music was a forum for expression, education, protest, and rebellion. It spoke to people experiencing life in the inner city. But it also spoke to people experiencing poverty, hardship, and all manner of oppression wherever they lived, and it ignited the spirit of youthful rebellion common to young people everywhere. By the time the new millennium rolled around, hip-hop music had moved beyond its inner-city roots to become some of the most popular music in the world. And Juelz Santana was about to join the business.

In the new millennium, hip-hop music is big, big business. It's no longer underground street music. Now it's part of popular entertainment all over the world. The extent to which individual artists like Juelz Santana continue to participate in hip-hop as a cultural movement is debatable. While hip-hop music as a whole has a rich and important social and political history, not every artist within that genre is concerned with making music that has any type of message. Music, after all, is not just about expression. It's also about entertainment.

There are many artists, of all types of music, who aren't at all concerned with political messages, educating their audience, or having any type of cause. They are entertainers, plain and simple, nothing more, nothing less. While some hip-hop artists could be seen as cultural educators and activists, others are entertainers. Where Juelz Santana fits in the spectrum is still unclear. In interviews he talks about keeping it real, making a difference, and being a voice for his generation. In his lyrics, however, he is often about the party. On one extreme, he has songs in which he raps about his love for his son. At the other extreme is a skit (on his first album) in which he pushes a girl out of his car after she vomits on him. To fans, it's entertainment. To critics, it's flat-out disgusting. To Juelz, it's just his brand of rap music.

From the 1920s until the 1940s, Harlem was a buzzing center of literary and musical culture. Time and white flight changed that. The arts were replaced by crime, drugs, violence, and gangs—fuel for the rhymes of Juelz Santana.

The Early Years

Juelz Santana was born on February 18, 1983, in New York City. He was named LaRon Louis James (he wouldn't take on his rap name until his teenage years). His parents were of African American and Dominican heritage. The family lived in Harlem, an area of the city with a rich history and culture.

Historic Harlem

Harlem was a great place for a budding rapper to grow and learn. It's an area of New York City with an amazing heritage. Dutch colonialists settled the area in 1658, but by the early twentieth century, it had become home to people of many different ethnicities. In the early years of the twentieth century, Harlem and other neighborhoods in Northern cities around America saw their black populations swell. What is now called the Great Migration was under way.

Racism was bad all over the United States, but it was especially widespread and violent in the South. By 1910, black people from the South were flooding the North in search of better jobs, better schools for their children, better lives, and greater equality. According to the article "The Great Migration" posted on *African American World* on pbs.org, more than one million black people moved north between 1910 and 1930.

As the black population of neighborhoods like Harlem grew, something never before seen began. In the North, many black people did find better jobs and gain access to education. For the first time, an educated black middle class began to form. With more education, money, and time, this new middle class was able to focus on developing art and culture like never before. The first distinct black literature took shape; blues music, jazz music, and the visual arts exploded; and a black intellectual movement pushed for advancement, recognition, and equal rights.

This cultural movement and celebration was largely focused in Harlem, and thus was called the "Harlem **Renaissance**." After many transformations, the Apollo Theater reopened its doors on Harlem's 125th Street and became the home of black music. It became an **icon** in black music and culture and a symbol of the Renaissance. It would one day host rap battles and be the place where Juelz Santana would have some of his first performances.

The Harlem Renaissance took place throughout the 1920s, 1930s, and into the 1940s when economic collapse and World War II brought hard times. After the war ended, Harlem, like many inner-city neighborhoods, went into a period of rapid decline. People fled the neighborhoods, buildings fell into disrepair, and crime rates skyrocketed in the following decades. Throughout the 1950s and1960s, however, Harlem's importance and influence continued, as it became a center of the civil rights movement. In 1968, a great riot spread through its streets after the murder of civil rights leader Dr. Martin Luther King Jr.

THE EARLY YEARS

By the 1960s, African Americans and others were fed up with the racism and prejudice they faced every day. Dr. Martin Luther King Jr. became the leader of the civil rights movement, which worked to bring equality to all. At the time of his assassination, he was working to fight poverty, because he believed it was the world's greatest oppressor.

The Downs and the Ups

Economic difficulties all over Harlem gave rise to drug abuse problems throughout the second half of the twentieth century. In the 1950s and 1960s, heroin use plagued the neighborhoods, and in the 1980s, a crack epidemic flared. But the news for Harlem wasn't all bad; in 1989, David N. Dinkins of Harlem became the first black man to be elected mayor of New York City.

After the violent eighties, Harlem began to see a shift. Throughout the 1990s, crime rates plummeted as the city's police force cracked down on Harlem neighborhoods. As the new millennium approached, Harlem was experiencing a rebirth or second renaissance as people began investing in its neighborhoods once again. This has continued. When former president Bill Clinton left the White House, he established his office in Harlem.

But Harlem's rebirth has not been beneficial to all. An article by Michael Powell for the *Washington Post* called the boom Harlem's "New Rush," and pointed out that while the movement is bringing new life to this historically and culturally rich area of the city, it is also forcing many of the poor and working-class black residents out. The cost of renting or buying a property in Harlem has increased so much that many of the area's long-time residents can no longer afford to live there.

Even with the changing times, however, Harlem remains a black cultural mecca. Columbia University's Web page, *Harlem History*, describes Harlem's importance as a center for art and culture over the last one hundred years:

> "Throughout the twentieth century, Harlem has served as the home and key inspiration to generations of novelists, poets, musicians, and actors. The pace of New York City, the blend of backgrounds of the people who settled in Harlem, and the difficulties associated

> with living in Harlem were among the experiences that found expression in theater, fiction and music, among other art forms."

After more than a century as an inspirational hub for artists of all genres, it should not be surprising that many of the artists of a new musical tradition, hip-hop, should come from Harlem. The difficulties the neighborhoods faced throughout the second half of the century—poverty, ghettoization, crime, drug abuse—would inspire much of the new music. Today this area of New York City boasts a long list of famous rappers who have come from its streets. Among them are Kurtis Blow, Doug E. Fresh, Freekey Zeekey, Damon Dash, Mase, Cam'ron, and of course, Juelz Santana.

Harlem Raps

Juelz Santana was a kid in Harlem in the 1980s, and he saw just how hard life could be, especially for black people in the inner city. He saw how the troubles of the ghetto could pull a young person into a life of gangs, drugs, and crime. He also saw how the inner city could inspire, and how some people turned to hip-hop music to deal with hardship. He saw, too, how hip-hop music could be a ticket out of the ghetto, for by the late eighties and early nineties, hip-hop artists were making it big, becoming famous, and getting rich.

By the time Juelz was twelve years old, he was writing rhymes about his world. He was also dreaming of being a big-time rapper. He was still a young teen when he got together with a friend and formed a rap duo called Draft Pick. They even signed a deal with Priority Records and began performing around New York City. Before long, they were on the stage of one of Harlem's most famous locales, performing at Amateur Night at the Apollo Theater. They won the competition two weeks in a row, and Juelz began earning a local reputation for his impressive freestyle abilities.

Not long after, Juelz got a big break. His cousin introduced him to a hip-hop artist named Cam'ron. Cam'ron was another Harlem rapper, and he was making a run for the big time. He had released his first album, *Confessions of Fire*, in 1998. When he met Juelz, Cam'ron was working on his second solo project.

Cam'ron was impressed with Juelz's lyrics, style, and flow. Within a week, he had the young rapper in the studio. He was going to put Juelz, a practical unknown, on his album.

The music world is very competitive, and few rappers make it without a hand from someone who has already found success. Juelz was no exception. Cam'ron heard Juelz rap and was impressed. Cam'ron gave the young artist's career a boost by putting Juelz on his next album.

In 1999, Juelz appeared as a featured guest on the singles "Double Up" and "All the Chickens." The songs were released on Cam'ron's second album *S.D.E.* (which stood for sports, drugs, and entertainment) in 2000. It would be another two years, however, before Juelz began getting any real notice in the music world.

First Props and the Dipset Crew

Much bigger things, however, were on the way. Juelz left Draft Pick behind to work with Cam'ron and pursue his own solo career. In 2002, Cam'ron released his third album, *Come Home with Me*, and it was his biggest success yet. Luckily for Juelz, the two singles that became huge hits, "Oh Boy" and "Hey Ma," also featured the young Santana. Cam'ron's fans loved the verses Juelz spit, and he started earning a fan base of his own. Juelz was finally getting props from the music world.

More recognition was on the way. In 2002, Cam'ron decided to found a rap crew, and he wanted Juelz on board. The two men joined up with Jim Jones, another Harlem MC, and the trio became The Diplomats. Soon, other Harlem-based rappers would join The Diplomats, and the crew would become better known as Dipset. Today they have a record label called Diplomat Records, and they've expanded their artist base to thirteen core members and numerous affiliates.

The very next year, on March 11, 2003, Dipset released its debut album, *Diplomatic Immunity*. As far as critical acclaim goes, it wasn't particularly well reviewed, but the two-disc album gave fans their first long look at Juelz, and they liked what they saw. Juelz was developing a serious following in New York City, particularly in the neighborhoods where he had grown up and performed. The album went *platinum*, and fans wanted more Santana. They would get it just a few months later with Juelz's own debut album, *From Me to U*.

Juelz Santana's solo debut album was a hit with his fans. Some of his songs were personal, giving his diehard fans a glimpse into the person behind the rhymes.

4

Out on His Own

On August 19, 2003, just five months after *Diplomatic Immunity* dropped, Juelz released his first solo album, *From Me to U*. The songs were a mixed bag of personal stories; coarse, gangsta rollicks and lighter club tunes. On the single "One Day I Smile," Juelz runs down a list of some of hip-hop's greatest MCs who have died. He names Tupac Shakur, Notorious B.I.G., Eazy-E, Jam Master Jay, and Big L, and says that he feels these great ones are reaching to him from the great beyond. He also raps that he believes God has chosen him for his hip-hop mission. In the single "Rain Drops," he speaks of some of the sorrows in his life, including his grandmother's fight with cancer.

It may seem strange to some listeners to hear the more-tender lyrics of a song like "Rain Drops" rapped alongside some of the other singles on the album. In the song "Jealousy," Juelz raps about assaulting a girlfriend on learning she's cheating. The song "Why" describes a man who actually enjoys running the streets and being part of a gang, saying, "They don't understand I love it and I like the beef/The war, the guns, the violence, it's all right with me." In an interview with nobodysmiling.com, however, Juelz described himself as a person with many different sides. He said that he brings many different experiences and multiple observations to his work, and that they are what make his music real:

> "I've been involved with the gangbanging [stuff], the regular street [stuff], but then I've managed to be a very family orientated type of [person] too. I love my family. I'm with my moms—I got a very close relationship with my moms, my brother, my [people]. You know what I'm saying? So I'm not just a one-sided [guy]—a gangbanging, violent [guy] to that point where that's all I care about. And I'm not just a family [guy] to the point where I'm just a soft, weak [guy] cause that's all I care about. I have so many different parts of life around me and just growing up, that I think it all comes out of me in my music."

In response to his new album, Juelz's fans became even more diehard. The album, overall, however, wasn't a huge seller, and Santana's fame remained a relatively regional affair. He took steps toward enlarging his image again the following year with the release of Dipset's second full-length album.

Although fans didn't get a solo album from Juelz in 2004, they did get the next Dipset drop, *Diplomatic Immunity II*. Some of the critical reviews of the album were better than for the first one, but the album didn't seem to create much

OUT ON HIS OWN 39

Violence is a major part of gangsta rap lyrics, and sometimes it spills over into the real world of the artists. Among those who have been murdered, many claim as a result of hip-hop feuds, are Notorious B.I.G., Jam Master Jay, and Tupac Shakur (shown in this photo).

of a stir in the hip-hop world. If fans were disappointed with the second Dipset effort, however, they had plenty of other opportunities to hear new stuff from Juelz. He's a king of the mixtape circuit, and in 2004 he pumped out plenty of music in these homemade recordings.

The Mixtape King

Juelz had released a mixtape called *Final Destination* back in 2003. In 2004, he began releasing a flurry of mixtapes to ramp up for his next solo album. Mixtapes have been a big part of hip-hop music practically from the beginning, but in recent years, artists have been increasingly relying on them as a type of **grassroots** marketing tool.

Mixtapes get their name from the decades-old practice of putting together a recording of songs from different artists. Like a playlist on an iPod, a mixtape is a personalized collection of music. Just about everyone who listens to music is familiar with the practice of making a workout mix, driving mix, party mix, love mix, or some other collection of songs that a person likes or that will be used for a specific purpose. When the practice first began, the recordings were called "mixtapes" because they were made on cassette tapes. Today, most mixtapes are not "tapes" at all. They are usually CDs, or even mp3 playlists, but the term mixtape still persists.

Mixtapes have a special place in hip-hop music. From the earliest years of hip-hop, artists made mixtapes of their music to sell on the street, often out of the trunk of a car. In fact, it was largely through these tapes being sold and passed around that hip-hop traveled from city to city and ignited a huge urban following. At that time, hip-hop was still too new, different, and "street" for the radio, so the music had to spread on the ground rather than on the airwaves. As rap got bigger, however, and artists began moving into real studios and putting out professionally produced records, the practice of making and selling mixtapes dropped away.

Today, the mixtape is enjoying a surge in popularity. Mixtapes are seen as a way to bring hip-hop music back once again to the streets of its birth. Artists feel that with mixtapes they can make a more personal connection with their audience, have a presence on the street, and generate interest in upcoming albums. And mixtapes, since they are usually homemade with low budgets and without the professional flare of a studio recording, tend not to be criticized for being too pop or commercial. In hip-hop today, mixtapes are becoming a way for rappers to reclaim street cred and legitimacy.

A typical hip-hop mixtape will contain some new work, as well as **remixes** of previous songs. Artists also frequently **collaborate** to make a mixtape. At one time, mixtapes were also defined by their length—they were much shorter than full-length albums. Today, that isn't necessarily the case at all. Sometimes artists put out mixtapes that are many times longer than a studio album would ever be.

The Next Stage

Between the release of his first and second solo albums, Juelz Santana sent three mixtapes to the street. The first, *Back Like Cooked Crack*, was released in late 2004. It contained twenty-seven songs and included features with Cam'ron and The Game. The second mixtape, *Back Like Cooked Crack 2: More Crack*, was released in early 2005. It also had twenty-six songs. Just a couple months after that, in the fall of 2005, he released yet another installment in the series, this one called *Back Like Cooked Crack 3: Fiend Out*. It had twenty-two songs. In just a year, Juelz had pumped more of his music onto the street than many artists put out in an entire career, and it was all just ramping up for his next drop, his second solo album.

In 2005, Juelz released his second studio album, *What the Game's Been Missing*. The album, however, nearly didn't make it through production. It was almost complete when disaster

Not all hip-hop music is released on high-quality CDs produced in fancy recording studios. Throughout hip-hop's history, mixtapes have played an important role in getting the music to the public, especially in the days when radio stations refused to play the music. They're still released today, but they're more professionally done.

OUT ON HIS OWN

struck. All the tracks were stored on a computer in the studio, and one day the hard drive crashed. In a panic, Juelz sent the computer to an expert repair shop, only to be told it couldn't be fixed. He got the same, devastating news from a number of other repair shops. It seemed all hope was lost. Then he sent the computer to a place in California. Miraculously, they were able to recover the files. The album was saved. When it hit the music stores, it did much better than Juelz's debut effort. It received more positive reviews and was certified platinum—a very, very big deal for any musical artist.

On his second album, Juelz hoped to show a deeper side and more thoughtful, complex lyrics. He definitely wanted to escape the "pop-gangsta" label that some critics gave him and give more meaning to his music. This effort produced the single "Rumble Young Man Rumble," in which Juelz describes growing up in a world where you have to fight for survival. It's one of the more personal songs on that album. An even more personal song came in the form of "Daddy," a surprisingly tender rap about all the things Juelz would do for his son. He also talks about his son in the single "Changes," saying that making a good life for his son is why he now raps:

> "now I got a lil son in my life
> That's the one in my life, that keeps me up in the night
> Writing these rhymes so he can live a comfortable life"

In an interview for nobodysmiling.com, Juelz talked about those personal songs as the most real and natural music that he makes:

> "[Those songs are] all about being real. What comes out is just what comes from my heart and what I'm

> thinking and what I'm feeling. It's not no format like I gotta think about it and cry about it for it to come out of me. It's there. It's real. It can't wait to come out actually, it's not even me. [Stuff] like that I can't control. I get in the studio and hear a beat and that [stuff] just genuinely starts rapidly pouring out. Like if you squeeze a wet sponge over a sink."

New Life

After *What the Game's Been Missing*, Juelz's fans were definitely feeling him. He was moving beyond his regional status, and his rising celebrity was opening new doors. In 2005, he was invited to perform as part of the Scream Tour at Madison Square Garden. In his interview with Tom Breihan for the *Village Voice*, Juelz said that performing in that famous venue was a dream come true:

> "That was the biggest thing ever for me, to come out at Madison Square Garden. I dreamt about that, something I always thought was real far-fetched. I still had a lot to accomplish just to get there, and to go out there and get the type of love I did, it let me know that I was definitely on the right path. I just need to keep people interested and keep people enjoying everything I do, and eventually I'll get to the level where I need to be. Not want to be, because I don't want to be nowhere. I feel like it's destined for me to be there. Some [people] are made to have money; some [people] are made to not. I'm made to start [stuff], man."

Juelz, however, isn't just focused on hip-hop music. One of the things that allows Juelz to be successful is that he has a very business-oriented mind. He's an entrepreneur, and one way he felt he could keep people interested was to branch out beyond music. So in February 2006, Santana launched his own clothing company called MAZIA (licensed by Z-line Clothing, Inc.). In going into fashion design, Juelz is participating in hip-hop's larger cultural traditions. From the beginning, hip-hop was never just about music. It was about lifestyles, and it contained music, dance, art, and inspired fashion and language. In an announcement placed on his Web site, Juelz

At one time or another, almost everyone has lost computer files to a malfunction (or mistakenly hitting the delete key). That can be an extremely stressful event. But if you're a rapper and those files are the songs for your next album—that can be a catastrophe. Just ask Juelz.

explained why he wants to be a player in the fashion world, that it's one more way he'll be keeping hip-hop "real":

"I want to be a driving force in the Urban Market. MAZIA will be a vengeance against all other brands

Juelz has joined the long line of hip-hop artists who have gotten into the fashion world. Pharrell Williams (shown in this photo) has his own line, and Juelz does too. But Juelz isn't new to fashion. His family owns a clothing store in Harlem.

OUT ON HIS OWN

that have taken the style from my generation and attempted to duplicate what we do naturally. Other labels have tried and just haven't gotten it right because they were missing that key ingredient . . . me."

With MAZIA, Juelz hopes to do for the fashion world what rap did for the music world. In the words of Lawrence Arthur of Z-Line Clothing, Juelz wants to hit the fashion world with the unique and vibrant creativity of the street:

"MAZIA's mission is to hit the fashion industry over the head with a look that is overzealous, powerful, and magnetic. We will provide a look that will give urban apparel what the game's been missing."

Juelz's move into fashion design, however, isn't really a leap into the unknown. His family has actually been connected to fashion for a long time. They own Santana's Town, a clothing store in Harlem, and Juelz still helps his mother run that family business. And his connection to the fashion world continued in 2007 when Juelz's music was featured on Nike's "Air Force One" commercial. Shortly after that, Juelz announced that he, his mother, and his aunt would be launching another clothing line called RoyElz. With Juelz's obvious desire to expand his audience, people wondered into what he would dip his toe next.

Though Juelz (shown here with a fan) is finding other areas, besides music, to get involved in, that doesn't mean the hip-hop world is about to lose one of its most-promising artists. Juelz plans to keep making music and pleasing his fans for a long time to come.

5
Still a Rapper

In 2005, Juelz Santana began branching out into another industry as well—movies. He headed to Philadelphia to shoot his first movie, *State Property* 2. It was a story about three gang leaders vying for control of Philadelphia's streets. Juelz warmed up to the acting world with a small role in the film.

Don't be confused, however, by Juelz's ventures into the business and acting worlds. He's not leaving his hip-hop music behind. In fact, even while starting his first fashion line, he was as busy as ever in the studio. In 2006, he dropped another mixtape. Called *Blow: The "I Can't Feel My Face" Prequel*, it was a collaboration with rapper Lil Wayne.

In many ways, the mixtape showed just how far Juelz Santana has come in the hip-hop world. Collaborating with an artist like Lil Wayne is no small thing; the Grammy-nominated artist is currently one of Southern rap's biggest stars. The mixtape also featured big names like Snoop Dogg, OutKast, and Young Jeezy, further evidence of how much Juelz's fame has increased.

Working Like an Addict

The twenty-six-song collaboration was so successful and in such high demand by fans that Juelz and Lil Wayne decided to do a complete studio album together. The much-anticipated album, called *I Can't Feel My Face*, was released in October 2007. The

Collaboration is a big part of hip-hop. In 2006, Juelz put out a mixtape with one of the biggest names in Southern rap, Lil Wayne. Fans were so enthusiastic about the result that the duo put out an album.

next mixtape in Santana's *Cooked Crack* series, *Black Like Cooked Crack 4: Rehab*, also came out in 2007.

If Juelz is addicted to anything, it has to be music and work. At the same time as he was gearing up for another big mixtape, he was hammering out songs in the studio for his third solo album. That album, *Born to Lose, Built to Win*, was also released in 2007. In an announcement posted on his Web site beforehand, Santana told fans what to expect when it came out:

> "This upcoming album will show my growth as an Artist. This time around, I'm talking about survival—maintaining my lifestyle and overcoming the obstacles and challenges life brings. The beats will be harder and the lyrics are tighter."

Juelz is quickly earning a reputation as one of the hardest working guys in the hip-hop industry. Among his upcoming projects is an album with Cam'ron. According to the current plans, it will be called *My Hood*. Although Juelz and Cam'ron have worked together many times, and are often featured artists on each other's singles, they've never done a whole album together. Dipset fans especially are anxious to see what they come up with.

On the Hollywood horizon, fans can keep their eyes open for two film projects as well. In 2007, filming wrapped up on *Killa Season 2*, which was written and directed by Cam'ron. Juelz also recently finished work on *The Project*, a movie about two white filmmakers who want to make a documentary about the inner city, expected out in 2008. Juelz is hoping that the future will bring even more opportunities like these. Nevertheless, for now, his main interest is still making music.

The Man's Motivation

In the music world, a record label can love you one minute, then drop you the next. One album can go multi-platinum, and the very next one can crash and burn. Fans can go crazy over you when you do one thing, and then trash you for changing or "selling out" when you try to do something different. To work so hard year after year in this industry, you have to love the music, and you have to have a lot of support and motivation.

In a December 2005 interview with hiphopcanada.com, Juelz talked about what motivates him and keeps him going. At the time of the interview, his son, LeRon James Junior, was just two years old, and Juelz said it was his son who inspires him the most. He also said that, after his son, it's the competition with other rappers that gets him fired up and makes him determined to constantly improve:

> "[My son inspires] everything [I do]. Once I had my son I knew I had to get on my grind. That's when I went and got my studio you know. . . . I just love watching him grow. . . . Musically it's got to be the competition [that inspires me]. There's always going to be competition out there so you know. . . . No matter what it's all about going forward; there's always more steps ahead. That's my motivation. There's always more out there and there's always going to be more out there."

In his interview with nobodysmiling.com, Juelz talked about another motivating factor: legacy. He said that he hoped, over time, he'd put his own unique mark on the music world, and he talked about how he would like to be remembered when he is done with the rap game:

> "[I'd like to be remembered] as a person who made a difference. Bottom line, if you are remembered, I feel like that is a good thing. Ya dig? But there are so many people that got lost in this game that it's just

STILL A RAPPER 53

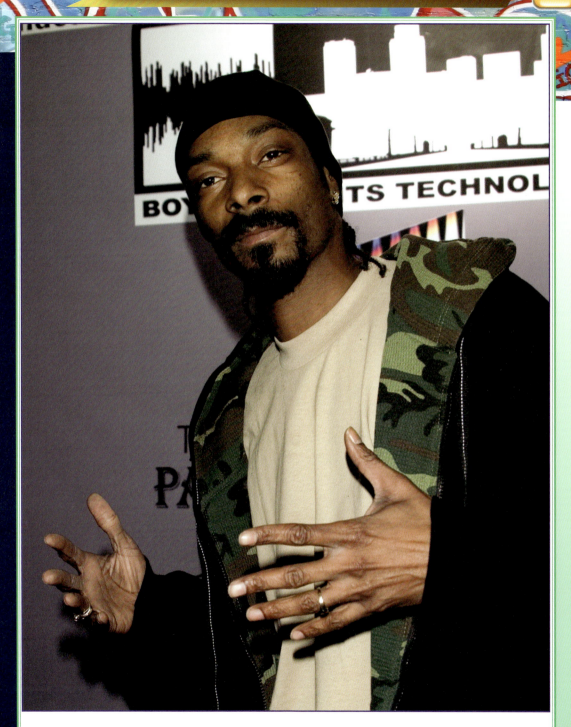

Juelz has also worked with Snoop Dogg. Snoop Dogg has been one of the biggest names in gangsta rap for many years. He is also one of the most controversial.

so hard to remember what's going on. If I could just leave a remembrance, that's good enough for me. You know what I'm saying? I know it ain't gonna be a bad one, because I ain't a bad [guy]. So bottom line, it's going to be everything I represent. As long as people remember me, they gon' remember."

There's no doubt that hip-hop is controversial. It always has been and probably will be. But one shouldn't brush all artists with the same brush. Groups like Public Enemy (Flavor Flav from the group is shown here) produce music that is politically and socially conscious.

It's a complicated wish for an artist in the rap world. After all, today hip-hop is in many ways better known for its controversial side—for the obscenity, the angry lyrics, the drugs, the gay-bashing and woman-bashing, the crime, and the bling—than for producing quality music that will endure through the ages. And yet, there certainly are those hip-hop artists who become legends. There are artists who make ground-breaking albums that will be remembered for their musical innovation (like Dr. Dre's *The Chronic*), there are artists whose albums will be remembered for their political and socially conscious messages (like Public Enemy's *It Takes a Nation of Millions to Hold Us Back*), and there are artists who will be remembered for careers filled with a spirit of revolution and protest (like rappers Tupac Shakur and KRS-One).

Juelz Santana is still young and has a lot more music on the way. Whether he will go down in history as one of these artists remains to be seen.

CHRONOLOGY

1920s   The Harlem Renaissance is in full swing.

1970s   Hip-hop is born in the Bronx section of New York City.

Feb. 18, 1983   LaRon Louis James, later known as Juelz Santana, is born in New York City.

2000   Juelz appears on Cam'ron's second album.

2002   Juelz appears on Cam'ron's third album.

2002   Juelz, Cam'ron, and Jim Jones form The Diplomats, later known as Dipset.

2003   Juelz releases the mixtape *Final Destination*.

Mar. 11, 2003   Dipset releases its debut album.

Apr. 19, 2003   Juelz's debut solo album is released.

2004   Dipset releases *Diplomatic Immunity II*.

2004   Juelz releases the mixtape *Back Like Cooked Crack*.

2005   The mixtapes *Back Like Cooked Crack 2: More Crack* and *Back Like Cooked Crack 3: Fiend Out* are released.

2005   Juelz's second solo album, *What the Game's Been Missing*, is released.

CHRONOLOGY

2005   Juelz performs at Madison Square Garden in New York City as part of the Scream Tour.

2005   Juelz acts in his first film, *State Property 2*.

2006   Juelz launches his own clothing company, MAZIA.

2006   Juelz releases another mixtape, *Blow: The "I Can't Feel My Face" Prequel*.

2007   Juelz's music is featured in a Nike ad.

2007   *I Can't Feel My Face*, Juelz and Lil Wayne's collaboration, is released.

2007   Juelz, his mother, and his aunt announce the launch of another clothing company, RoyElz.

2007   Juelz releases another mixtape, *Back Like Cooked Crack 4: Rehab*.

2007   *Born to Lose, Built to Win*, Juelz's third solo album, is released.

2007   Juelz costars in *Killa Season 2*.

2008   *The Project*, a film costarring Juelz, is released.

Accomplishments and Awards

Albums

2003 *From Me to U*

2005 *What the Game's Been Missing*

2007 *Born to Lose, Built to Win*

DVD

2005 *Fabolous—Twista & Juelz Santana on DVD*

Films

2005 *State Property 2*

2007 *Killa Season 2*

2008 *The Project*

Books

Bogdanov, Vladimir, Chris Woodstra, Steven Thomas Erlewine, and John Bush (eds.). *All Music Guide to Hip-Hop: The Definitive Guide to Rap and Hip-Hop.* San Francisco, Calif.: Backbeat Books, 2003.

Chang, Jeff. *Can't Stop Won't Stop: A History of the Hip-Hop Generation.* New York: Picador, 2005.

Emcee Escher and Alex Rappaport. *The Rapper's Handbook: A Guide to Freestyling, Writing Rhymes, and Battling.* New York: Flocabulary Press, 2006.

George, Nelson. *Hip Hop America.* New York: Penguin, 2005.

Kusek, Dave, and Gerd Leonhard. *The Future of Music: Manifesto for the Digital Music Revolution.* Boston, Mass.: Berkley Press, 2005.

Light, Alan (ed.). *The Vibe History of Hip Hop.* New York: Three Rivers Press, 1999.

Waters, Rosa. *Hip-Hop: A Short History.* Broomall, Pa.: Mason Crest, 2007.

Watkins, S. Craig. *Hip Hop Matters: Politics, Pop Culture, and the Struggle for the Soul of a Movement.* Boston, Mass.: Beacon Press, 2006.

FURTHER READING/INTERNET RESOURCES

Web Sites

Juelz Santana on Def Jam
www.defjam.com/site/artist_home.php?artist_id=518

Juelz Santana on MySpace
www.myspace.com/juelzsantana

Santana's Town
www.santanastown.com

Glossary

collaborate—Work with others to create a product.

culture—The beliefs, customs, practices, and social behavior of a particular nation or people.

entrepreneur—Someone who sets up and finances new businesses to make a profit.

ethnic—Relating to a person or to a large group of people who share a national, racial, linguistic, or religious heritage.

genre—A category into which a work of art can be placed based on its form, media, or subject.

grassroots—The ordinary people of a community.

homophobic—Possessing an unrealistic fear of homosexuality and homosexuals.

icon—Someone widely and uncritically admired as a symbol of a movement or field.

mainstream—The ideas, actions, and values that are most widely accepted by a group or society.

mixtapes—Compilations of songs recorded from other sources.

oppression—The domination of a person or group of people.

GLOSSARY

platinum—A designation indicating that a recording has sold one million units.

R&B—Rhythm and blues; a style of music combining elements of blues and jazz, and originally developed by African Americans.

remixes—Re-recordings.

Renaissance—A revival of skills, arts, and culture.

underground—Separate from the prevailing social or artistic environment.

Index

"All The Chickens" 35
Apollo Theatre, the 33

Back Like Cooked Crack 41
BB King 20
break dancing 23
Bronx, the 22

Cam'ron 34
Clinton, Bill 32
Come Home with Me 35
Confessions of Fire 34

Dinkins, David N. 32
Diplomat Records 10

Diplomatic Immunity 35
Diplomatic Immunity II 38
Dipset 35
　as "The Diplomats" 35
"Double Up" 35
Draft Pick 33

Final Destination 40
From Me to U 35

Great Migration 29

Harlem 29
　drugs 32
　hip-hop artists 33

INDEX

"New Rush" 32
Renaissance 30
and World War II 30
"Hey Ma" 35
hip-hop
   Bronx roots of 22–25
   East Coast 12
   freestyle rap 23
   gangsta rap 12–13
   mixtapes 40–41
   as resistance and protest 21–22
   West Coast 11
Holiday, Billie 22

Ice-T 12

James, La Ron Louis (see Santana, Juelz)
Jones, Jim 35

King, Martin Luther Jr. 30

Meeropol, Abel 22
mixtapes 10, 40

N.W.A 12

"Oh Boy" 35
"One Day I Smile" 37

premiere 10
Priority Records 33

"Rain Drops" 37

Santana, Juelz
   as a businessman 9–10
   as "Pop-gangsta" 12
   inspirations of 37
   on "Keeping it Real" 16
S.D.E 35
"Strange Fruit" 22

tagging 23–25
Tupac Shakur 37, 39

Village Voice 15

"Why" 38

About the Author

Author Janice Rockworth grew up in the eighties when hip-hop music was just gaining momentum on the popular music scene. She remembers as a child being shocked by the lyrics of early hip-hop group 2 Live Crew, and amused by the light-hearted music of DJ Jazzy Jeff and the Fresh Prince. After studying sociology at an all-women's college, she became interested in hip-hop's social, historical, and political significance. Today she is a fan of political, conscious, and other alternative hip-hop styles.

Picture Credits

Corbis: front cover
istockphoto: p. 17
   Cech, Marek: p. 45
   duncan1890: p. 18
   Leão, Abel: p. 24
   terraxplorer: p. 28
   Trigg, Susan: p. 11
Jupiter Images: p. 42
Library of Congress: pp. 26, 31
PR Photos: p. 34
   Bielawski, Adam: pp. 2, 8, 20, 36, 50
   Gabber, David: p. 54
   Harris, Glenn: pp. 14, 46
   Hatcher, Chris: p. 53
   Thompson, Terry: p. 39

To the best knowledge of the publisher, all other images are in the public domain. If any image has been inadvertently uncredited, please notify Harding House Publishing Service, Vestal, New York 13850, so that rectification can be made for future printings.